Jennifer
Romeika

Tanner

Ramaika

Life in the Great Ice Age

by **Michael** and **Beverly Oard**

Edited by **Gloria Clanin**

Illustrated by

Earl and Bonita Snellenberger

Table of Contents

Preface

Come along with us as we travel to a time long ago when the world was very different than it is now. Our story takes place toward the end of the Great Ice Age in what is now central Europe. A small group of people have settled in a valley with several caves in its sides. These caves served as protection from the fierce winds and the wild animals that lived in the valley.

We will spend a summer with 11-year-old Jabeth and his tribe, living near a great Ice-Age glacier. The summer season had to be spent preparing for the long, cold winter, which came very early. Provisions needed to be gathered before the snow set in, or it would be difficult to hunt game. Blizzards lasted many days, and travel of any kind was impossible.

Many people are confused about what "cave men" have to do with the Bible. Where do they fit? Or do they belong at all? They are the descendants of Noah's sons, Ham, Shem, and Japheth. After God confused languages at the Tower of Babel, the people spread out all over the world (Genesis 11:1–9).

These were not the backward and ignorant savages usually depicted in books or movies. They were the descendants of people who built cities, herded livestock, played musical instruments, and made tools of bronze and iron (Genesis 4:17–22). The Ark, built by Noah and

his sons, was huge, and survived the greatest and longest storm the earth has ever seen. The Tower of Babel was an incredible engineering feat. No, these were not savages, but descendants of men who were intelligent and skilled.

After the languages were confused, people who spoke the same language formed into groups. These groups, because they spoke different languages, separated and went in different directions. As the "families" grew larger and larger, they separated into new families. As these new families traveled farther and farther, their languages gradually changed, as did their life-styles. Each family group had to learn how to survive in the land where they had migrated.

Of interest is that, as the tribes developed into very different cultures, they carried with them stories of the great Flood and the one true God.

The family units—called tribes or clans—who traveled north, had to deal with colder climates. One group of people, known as the Neanderthals, were once mistakenly thought by some to be primitive apemen because of their brutish appearance. We now know that they were true men, most likely suffering from rickets and arthritis caused by the cold, dark climate of the world after the Flood.

In our story, the Beetle-Brows are Neanderthals. They were given the name

"Neanderthal" because the first Neanderthal bones were found in the Neander valley in Germany.

Jabeth's tribe are the people we call Cro-Magnon. These people were named after a cave in the Dordogne district of France, where their remains have been found.

As the families began to develop different cultures, they also began to develop physical features unique to each group. At first the family groups—therefore the gene pools—were fairly small. Traits such as skin color, hair texture, body build, temperament, etc., became dominant within each group. This was the beginning of what we call the different "races." However, there is really only one race—the human race.

The entire world could easily have been populated in a few hundred years. It did not take millions of years, as many believe. In recent years, archaeology has confirmed that many civilizations appeared about the same time, only a few thousand years ago. Highly developed civilizations sprang up all over the world, after short periods spent hunting and gathering.

A pattern seems to have occurred over and over after the Ice Age. When a tribe moved to a new area, they looked for a temporary location to set up camp. Then they searched for a more permanent site for their village or city. Archaeologists have mistaken these temporary sites as evidence of a "stone-age culture."

Temporary homes could have been made of stones, hides, or sticks; even caves were still used. The people would need time to find out if an area could support them. Would there be enough water and game? Would the ground be fertile enough to grow their crops? If they were skilled at working with metals, they would need time to search for veins of ore. This might take years, and in the meantime the tribe had to survive off the land as best they could. They hunted, fished, and gathered fruits and nuts. Some groups have continued this style of living up to the present time.

Protection became a very important issue: not only from wild animals, but now men also feared other men. As the tribes developed, some had become warlike, while others preferred a life of farming and caring for their animals.

Some tribes became great nations. They captured the best sites for their big cities and built large armies. Some tribes preferred rural areas, while others, not able to survive, died out.

The nomadic tribes carried articles from one area to another over great distances. Trade routes soon sprang up, and people began the difficult task of learning other languages.

It must have been a frightening time for the people who lived during the Ice Age, because so many changes were taking place. The climate was going through drastic changes. They didn't know what the future would hold. Where would they live? Would there be enough food? Would they be able to survive in a harsh world?

Part I — Chapter 1
Survival in a Harsh World

The scream of an enraged saber-toothed tiger pierced the stillness of the night. Jabeth, jolted out of a deep sleep, sprang up to a sitting position as a shiver of fear went down his spine. Thar, ready to defend his master, began snarling and tried to lunge toward the cave entrance. Jabeth quickly put an arm around the shaggy neck of his wolf dog to calm him.

Grandfather was already on his feet throwing more wood on the fire. The fire was all that separated them from the pacing tiger. The tiger turned and disappeared into the blackness of the night. Jabeth felt safe. The tiger would stay away for the rest of the night.

Jabeth lay back down and burrowed deeply into his warm animal furs. A stream lay outside the cave, and many animals would come there to drink at night. The saber-toothed tiger the children called "the old-toothed one" often hunted antelope and reindeer by the stream. Sometimes he would climb the slope leading to the cave, but the fire near the entrance would keep him out. Tonight, he would seek easier prey elsewhere and leave Jabeth and his family alone.

Daily Life

Many thoughts wandered through Jabeth's mind as he lay waiting for sleep to come. "This was one of the best days I've ever had. I trapped and killed my first rabbit; it was delicious. Father was very impressed with my hunting skill.

"It was fun helping Father dig a pit trap, yesterday. It was hard work and took all day. I hope an antelope or reindeer falls into it.

"Grandfather said there was a time when we didn't need to preserve food for winter. The weather was warm all year around. It must have been wonderful with no cold snow or freezing nights. I can hardly wait for Grandfather to tell us more of what it was like. Grandpa is so wise; he knows just about everything. He's been through many hunts and is very brave." A feeling of comfort stole over Jabeth as he drifted off into dreams of life before the cold.

The next day, Jabeth could hardly wait for the sun to set so Grandpa could start telling stories.

Grandfather was his favorite story teller. Evenings by the cave fire were special times. With the fire close to the cave entrance and the strong walls around them, they felt entirely safe. Ten fur tents lined its walls and kept them warm in the clammy cave. Five tents lined one side and five were on the other. Two adults or three children slept in each tent. The cave walls were equal to the combined height of five men. Columns of rock, covered with black soot, reached down to the floor in the back of the cave. Small tunnels led off the main cave room into small chambers where the children loved to play.

From his cliff home, Jabeth looked down on the grass blowing in waves across the plain. A few scrubby trees dotted the landscape. Jabeth saw a herd of reindeer grazing in the distance. The sun was slowly sinking behind the hills. The sky displayed a brilliant array of reds and oranges. Winters might be very cold, but the summers were very beautiful.

Grandfather Tells of Noah's Ark

It was time for Grandfather to begin story telling. The children always looked forward to story time around the cave fire. Jabeth had helped the women gather wood for the fire. Mother and Myra, his older sister, had already served the food and cleaned the eating area.

Everyone took their places. Jabeth sat on his special rock across from Grandfather. Thar laid his chin on Jabeth's leg. Jabeth had raised him from a puppy. Thar never left his side; he was a faithful friend.

Grandfather looked fondly across at his red-haired grandson. He remembered Jabeth's father when he was young; both were alike, full of life and curiosity.

"Grandfather, how did we come to live in this valley?" Jabeth asked.

Jabeth waited with excitement until Grandfather took a deep breath, signaling he was ready to begin a story. Grandfather shifted his old body so that his hunting wounds from his ancient enemy, the cave bear, wouldn't hurt as much. The wounds were still bothering him after all these years. He smiled at his family and began the story.

"Long, long ago, before Noah's Flood, there was a time when evil was all over the land.

People hated God and His rules and wanted to make their own rules. This made God very sad and disappointed. So He decided to clean the earth of all men except our great ancestor, Noah, his three sons, and their wives. They loved and obeyed God. God may have wondered if harsher weather and a shorter growing season would cause the people to ask Him for help. He hoped they would understand that everything good comes from Him. Then they would be better, happier people and not fight so much."

Jabeth interjected, "But Grandfather, we love God and know everything good comes from Him."

"Yes," Grandfather replied, "but there are many people who still do not understand that God wants good for them and not evil. Your great ancestor, Japheth, Noah's son, told this story to his son, and so it was passed down through the generations. As I was saying, God decided to clean the earth by sending a Great Flood."

The Great Flood

God told Noah and his sons to build a large boat which they called the Ark. They needed to prepare for the Flood that would cover the whole earth. Noah, Japheth, Ham, and Shem believed God and built an enormous barge-like boat on dry land. They worked hard for many years. Their neighbors laughed at them. They called the boat Noah's folly. Noah told them about God's plan, but they still laughed. How sad Noah and his family must have been because their neighbors did not listen.

"Then the animals came to Noah, two of each kind, for protection as God had ordered. The animals seemed to sense danger in the air and went into the boat. The animals stayed on the lower decks. Your ancestor, Japheth, after whom you were named, and all his family lived on the upper deck. When everything was ready, God shut the door to the Ark. Soon the rain came down, at first softly; and then harder. It sounded like hundreds of carpenters pounding on the roof.

"An even louder noise startled Noah and his family. They heard rumblings that seemed to begin deep in the ground. They climbed up to peek out through the window at the top of the Ark. What they saw frightened them. Water shot up into the air from everywhere. The little spring near their home was gushing like a fountain. Their neighbors' wells were shooting water high into the sky.

"Suddenly, they felt a jolt; the boat rocked back and forth. They were floating! How grateful they were that they had listened to God and were safe in the boat rather than outside!

"The animals in the Ark grew quieter and quieter. The wild movement of the boat was rocking them to sleep! Japheth was seasick from the motion. The smell of sulfur was suffocating. He wondered where it was coming from. He looked outside and saw in the distance what looked like an enormous fountain of fire. Rocks began bouncing off the roof of the Ark. He was glad God had told them to build a strong Ark.

"Each day Japheth marked a notch on the wall of the Ark. Finally, after 150 days of tossing on the water, they landed on a mountain they called Ararat. After 221 more days, Japheth, his parents, two brothers, and their wives left the Ark."

13

Entering the "New World"

Noah and his family were thankful to God for protecting them, and they were glad the Flood was over. They made an altar and offered a sacrifice of thanksgiving to God. A rainbow arched across the sky. There had been nothing, before the Flood, that could rival its beauty. Its colors shifted from the majesty of purple to the delicacy of pink. It was the first rainbow man had ever seen. Noah heard God promise to never again send a horrible Flood. It was wonderful to be alive.

"The mountain was cold and windy. From the valley, they saw their first snow, capping the mountains all around. The land as far as they could see was barren. There were no trees, animals, or birds. The sky was dim. Most days, there was a thick haze obscuring the sun and stars. Branches and sticks protruded from the bare ground. Some of them had green sprouts growing from them. Olive shoots were common. Grass had sprung up here and there. Japheth had saved seeds and was eager to plant them.

"Noah and his sons lived at the foot of the mountain until the land became green and herds of animals once again roamed. From the position of the stars, Noah figured that they had drifted in a northerly direction. If they traveled south, they hoped to eventually find their old home. But that was not to be. As they journeyed south, the terrain looked strange because the land had changed. The mountains were much larger than they remembered. After several moons of searching without success, they settled in a beautiful land between two large rivers. They named them Tigris and Euphrates, after the two mighty rivers that had flowed near their home before the Flood. The soil in the new area was rich and they could grow all the food they would need.

"Since the time of Noah's Flood, the ground has been unsettled and sometimes shakes. During much of the time since the Flood, ash has hidden the sun. Ash was especially thick after the rumbling of fire mountains, like the one our ancestors first saw before the Ark floated. Dust and ash would often fall from the sky. When the ash clouds were thick, the air turned colder, there was more snow and rain. When the ash cleared, the sun shone brightly. It warmed the earth and brought less snow and rain. I believe, Jabeth, that these dark ash clouds have caused the cold and the Great Wall of Ice."

The cave fire dimmed, casting eerie shadows on the jagged walls. Grandfather rose to add more wood as the nights were getting cooler. Father, Mother, Myra, and Jabeth said their evening prayers together. After telling each other good night, they settled quietly into their comfortable fur beds. Jabeth fell asleep with his faithful dog, Thar, by his side.

Chapter 2
The Beetle-Brow People

The next afternoon Jabeth and his cousin, Baylock, were climbing trees. They were racing each other to the top when Jabeth heard Baylock yelling, "I see people coming our way; look over there toward the hills!" Jabeth looked with alarm. The boys quickly shinnied down the trunk and raced to tell Jabeth's father, Lathan. He was the head of the tribe and would tell the others what to do. Lathan told the women and children to hurry into their caves for safety. Some tribes that wandered came to kill and steal; although most were friendly, Lathan was never sure what to expect. The women and children hid until the leaders could learn the strangers' intentions.

Jabeth remembered the last spring thaw, when another tribe had wandered through. They weren't nice, but had pretended to be friendly. Jabeth's tribe invited them to sleep in the cave. In the middle of the night, they quietly stole food and left. Thar hadn't barked. Maybe they'd fed him some dried mammoth meat.

When everyone awoke the next morning, Father was very angry. He and the other men gathered their spears and clubs. They chased the thieves for half a day before catching up to them. Jabeth and the other boys went along. They made a lot of noise by banging on hollow sticks and yelling. Father, Naboth, and all the other men were painted with a red paint called ocher. They'd been so fierce-looking and angry that the guilty ones dropped the food and ran. Jabeth hoped the approaching tribe would be friendly so he could have some fun.

Now, Jabeth's father and Grandfather and a few other men cautiously approached the new tribe. The rest of the men were hiding in ambush in case Lathan needed them. Jabeth, as well as everyone else in his tribe, was prepared to fight. Ever since Jabeth could remember, they had prepared stashes of rocks for protection from wild animals or enemies. They planned to throw the rocks down from their caves onto any unfriendly invaders. Father and Grandfather, who was the interpreter, talked a long time to the leaders of the strange tribe. Then they all turned and walked together toward the cave. Jabeth's tribe let out a sigh of relief. They were glad they didn't have to fight, but could they trust the strangers?

Now that the new tribe was closer, Jabeth noticed that they didn't look the same as his people. The men were shorter and heavier than Jabeth's father. Their foreheads weren't as high as Mother and Myra's, but were sloped and they had lumps above their eyes. Their chins disappeared into their necks. Lathan turned and waved to the men who were hiding. Later, Grandfather told Jabeth that the tribe was called the Beetle-Brows. They had passed through our valley five years ago. Grandfather said that they were friendly, good hunters, and honest. He said they had traded berries for meat in the past, and that the tribes had shared hunting techniques. Jabeth was excited to learn more about the strangers' ways. He learned they'd probably stay for at least a moon.

Jabeth and his friends felt a little shy and afraid because the strangers looked different. As the boys peered down from their place of safety, they saw the children from the Beetle-Brow clan target practicing. The Beetle-Brow children were throwing spears at a small hide that they had attached to a tree limb. They were chattering happily among themselves. Once in a while Jabeth recognized a word or two. One of the new boys noticed Jabeth and his friends watching, so he waved. Perhaps the Beetle-Brows weren't so strange after all. Jabeth and his friends longed to play with them. They climbed down from their perch and stood waiting for an invitation. In a moment all the children were happily playing together.

Learning About Each Other

That afternoon some boys from both tribes were playing one of their favorite games, "drag the snake." Teams of two boys raced each other, pulling logs with braided leather ropes. Other boys were playing a game they called "crack the egg." One of the boys would push an egg-shaped rock along the ground. The other boys tried to take it away from him with their sticks before he could roll the rock into a small hole dug for the game.

Jabeth saw that Lathan wasn't busy, so he asked his father why the Beetle-Brow clan looked so different from the neighboring tribes.

"We are all different in some ways," Father answered. "The short, strong men with sloping foreheads make up many tribes. Remember Grandpa told you that long ago all people were one large tribe, but we had to leave the beautiful Tigris-Euphrates Valley? We broke into family groups. The Beetle-Brow clan was one of those groups. The family tribes wandered in many different directions after our language became confused. Beetle-Brows came to live here long before we arrived. They lived in caves just south of the Great Wall of Ice, but they moved away many, many moons ago. Occasionally, how their legs became bowed and their foreheads sloped.

"Grandfather said the tribes that lived in sunnier areas didn't change as much. Eating too much meat and not enough roots and berries may have also changed their appearance. Many times when the people went out hunting, their bones would break easily and they would die. It was a difficult time for their people. The once mighty Beetle-Brow tribe, so proud of their strength and number, became fewer and fewer. Now that the sun shines more often, they are becoming stronger and healthier. They have more contact with other tribes now, and they marry outside their tribe more. This may help, too. As you can see, the younger men are straighter and more like us than their parents."

Jabeth was glad that the Beetle-Brow tribe was becoming healthier. He liked his new friends. In spite of their sufferings, the tribe was a cheerful group.

Beetle-Brow hunters still pass through our area following the reindeer and bison herds. The women and children accompany the men to help with the butchering and skinning.

"The Beetle-Brow's story is sad. Once they were a large tribe. When they came to this land, it was dark most of the time because the sky was filled with ash. It rained and snowed often. Because of the miserable weather, men hunted near their caves. Over the years, their bodies changed. Grandfather thinks those long dark days and living in caves caused the peoples' bones to soften. Maybe that's

Preparation for the Hunt

The next morning, when Jabeth woke he was eager to start the day. He saw that his parents were still sleeping and knew he was not to awaken them. He could see the sky beginning to lighten. Everyone should wake up soon, and he wished they would hurry. This was the day of the cave-bear hunt. It would take at least ten strong, brave men to drive the bear out of its cave and kill it. Two moons ago, it had wounded and nearly killed one of the men. As the warm season wore on, the cave bear was becoming more and more aggressive and dangerous. The women were now afraid to hunt berries on the hillside because they feared the beast. Father and a few of the men from the neighboring caves were going to destroy the cave bear before it killed someone.

This would be the first time Jabeth's father had allowed him to go on a dangerous hunt with the men. Jabeth knew that if the fight went wrong he would have to run for safety. He was the fastest runner among his friends, and was proud that his father had noticed. Jabeth prayed God would protect all of the men from the sharp teeth and claws of the cave bear and give them a safe hunt.

Finally, Mother rose to prepare breakfast for the family. She first built a fire to heat her cooking rocks. She would cook breakfast on the flat rocks when they were hot enough. Then, Mother made a mixture of ground nuts, bulbs, and ptarmigan bird eggs. She stirred the ingredients until they were thoroughly mixed and carefully shaped them into flat patties. Then she began baking them on the heated rocks. The delicious smell woke Father and the rest of the family.

While Mother finished preparing breakfast, Father and some of the other men continued to prepare for the cave bear hunt. They wanted their weapons to be sharp and strong. Gripping an egg-shaped stone, Father used it as a hammer to knock flakes from a large piece of flint. When shaped and sharpened, these flakes would make fine spear points. Tiny chips were carefully removed from the flakes by hammering gently with the tip of an antler point. The flint flakes gradually became perfectly shaped spearpoints. Little by little the spearpoints were thinned down until their edges were sharp and penetrating. The finished points were lashed with lacings of animal thong to strong wood shafts. These spears would be lethal weapons in the hunt for the fierce cave bear.

It was time for breakfast. Once the patties were cooled, Mother topped each with crushed gooseberries before serving. After thanking God for their delicious meal, the family ate quickly, then gathered outside.

The sun was beginning to warm the earth. A light mist was rising from the ground. The sky was clear and losing its gray hue. It was a beautiful day. Three of the men from the Beetle-Brow clan asked if they could join in the hunt. They were expert hunters. Excitement ran high. The night before, the men had talked and planned for hours about how they were going to kill the bear. Now was the time to put their plan into action.

Battle with the Cave Bear

Lathan, his men, and some of the Beetle-Brows set out toward the other side of the valley where the cave bear had its lair. Each man felt excitement and fear at the same time. How would the battle come out? Would they escape unharmed?

Three men climbed the cliff overhanging the cave. Quietly, they gathered large stones to drop on the bear's head. Jabeth watched from a clump of scrubby trees. He wondered how the men planned to get the bear to come out of its den. As he was watching, some men slowly sneaked to the front of the dark entrance. They built a large pile of moss and sticks. One of the men had brought fire. They were going to smoke the bear out! Jabeth saw his father, Naboth, and some other men standing ready with their spears.

Zorak lit the fire. The air filled with smoke, but just then the wind shifted! It was blowing the wrong way! Gath, Soren, and Zorak grabbed some skin blankets and waved the smoke back toward the entrance of the cave. Some Beetle-Brow men were throwing rocks into the cave to drive the sleeping bear out. Soon the bear lumbered out, and it was furious! Its mean, beady eyes were red and watering from the smoke. The tall bruin rose on its hind legs and towered over the men. The men waiting above the cave threw stones down on the bear's head. Instead of knocking him out, the rocks only made the cave bear angrier.

Gath ventured closer, looking for an opening, and tried to spear the bear's side. The bear swung around and knocked him off his feet, scratching him across the chest with its claws. Three Beetle-Brow men jumped toward the bear—one to divert him and two to drag Gath away. Jabeth could feel his heart pounding.

Soren quickly threw his spear into the bear's side. Jabeth's father threw a spear at the bear's throat, and one of the men above dropped another large stone on its head. The spear hit first; then the rock struck. The bear was dazed for a moment, then clumsily staggered toward the men, growling and clawing at them. The tribesmen scattered in all directions. The angry bear made an enraged swipe at Zorak, barely missing him. Then one of the Beetle-Brow men threw a well-aimed spear at its heart. As the bear reeled, Lathan quickly ran up to it and plunged another spear into his chest. It fell down with a thud, driving the two spears deep into its body. Finally, the bear stopped moving. Soren took a knife and cut its throat while the other men watched from a distance. Soren ran quickly away, glancing back to make sure the bear was really dead.

Together, the men built a sled of poles to carry the bear. Ten of the strongest men pulled the animal into camp. Tonight they would eat well as they celebrated their victory! Lathan would be honored since he threw the fatal spear. Jabeth felt he was going to burst with pride. The hunt had taken great courage. There would be dancing and retelling of brave exploits.

As the men neared the camp, the women and children ran out to inspect the huge bear. The women praised the men as the younger children jumped around the bear and pretended to spear it with their sticks. Everyone was glad there hadn't been any serious injuries. Soon quick work was made of skinning the bruin. The hide was huge and would make a wonderful blanket.

The women attended to Gath's wound. It wasn't deep, but he would have scars to show as a badge of courage to his children and grandchildren.

Celebrating the Hunt

Everyone prepared for the feast. While the boys gathered wood for the bonfire, the girls went to dig roots to flavor the meat. The women were chatting merrily as they prepared the cave-bear stew.

Some of the men cleared the area around the cave fire for dancing. The warriors who had been on the hunt decorated their bodies with red ocher paint. The old men tightened their drums and practiced playing their reed pipes. It was a happy time.

As the smell of food filled the cave, Jabeth's mouth began to water. Just then, Lathan called everyone to eat. They praised God for the meal of bear meat and thanked Him for protection during the hunt. The excitement of the day's hunt had given them huge appetites and they dug in ravenously. The cave bear stew was the tribe's favorite food. It contained bog beans, lake reeds, various root tubers, and a few beetles for seasoning. Soon all the people were full and content.

As the sun started to set and the air grew chilly, everyone gathered around the fire. The fire licked high toward the top of the cave. Drums began beating at a slow, lazy pace and then became faster and faster.

Lathan, Gath, Soren, and the rest of the men who had been on the hunt jumped up at the same time. They began to dance and stab their spears at the bear's skin draped over a rock. As they danced they chanted their hunting song. Ungar, the leader of the Beetle-Brow people, and some of the other men wore bear pelts over their heads and backs. These pelts were prized treasures of past hunts.

24

When the song ended, Grandfather told the story of the day's hunt. His voice kept time with the flute and drums. Grandfather was very proud of his son and all the men who had risked their lives. He sat very straight and spoke long and splendidly of the men's bravery and the huge bear's anger. The listeners "ooed and ahhhed" with admiration. This tale would be told again and again around evening campfires. When the story had been told, the dancers began their dancing all over again. Then the rest of the men and boys jumped into the circle and joyfully danced. All the people praised the Lord for the successful hunt.

26

Preparing the Bear Hide and Meat

Morning came quickly. There would be no major excitement today. Now began the work of preparing the cave bear meat and hide for winter. The women scraped the fat off the bear's stretched hide, then smeared a mixture of brains and liver on it to soften and tan the leather. They would leave this mixture on for several days and then wash it off.

Several women put meat into deep, cool earth pits for storage. Others cut bear meat into strips with a burin and laid them on drying racks.

In a corner of the cave, Myra and her friend, Zilo, placed bear stew in a shallow "bowl" in the ground which they had lined with hide. Stones were heated and dropped into the cooking bowl. It took a long time to cook this way. When the first rocks cooled off, Myra would take them out and Zilo would add more.

Chapter 3
Confusion of Languages

While Jabeth finished his chores, a gust of cold wind blew from the direction of the Great Ice Wall. He knew the warm season was nearly over. Jabeth shivered. Noticing that Grandfather was alone, Jabeth asked him a question.

"Grandfather, why does our tribe live in such a cold place?" As they walked over to sit on a nearby rock, Grandfather began to tell his story. "A long time ago, our ancestors lived in a warm, beautiful valley. Life was easy. Then Noah's grandchildren and great-grandchildren felt so important they didn't think they needed God.

"They knew the world had been punished for disobedience by God's Flood, but they still refused to honor and serve Him. What they wanted seemed more important to them than what God wanted. They decided to create gods that would allow them to do as they pleased. They turned away from the Creator and began to worship the stars He had created. They built a high tower so they could stand closer to the stars they worshiped.

"God saw that there was no end to their evil. To prevent them from continuing in such ways, He confused their language, so they could no longer understand each other. There was so much confusion, they stopped work on the tower. They soon mistrusted anyone they couldn't understand. Fights broke out. Since they could not live in peace, the people divided into small groups that spoke the same language, and left the warm Tigris- Euphrates Valley. That's how God scattered people to distant lands all over the earth.

"Our family sought a new land with better hunting grounds. We looked for a place of beauty and peace. We headed toward the North Star. Our family would settle in an area for a while, then pack up and move on. We moved with the herds of animals, hunting and gathering roots and berries as we went. Sometimes we lived in valleys surrounded by tall mountains. A few mountains spit out fire and smoke.

One time we thought we would all die. A black wall of ash rose from a nearby mountain and covered the sun. The ash fell all around us; it was hard to breathe. We remembered God and prayed to Him for help. The sun was covered for three moons. We went deep into a nearby cave, where He protected us from harm. When the smoke thinned, we built an altar to God and thanked Him for sparing our lives.

"As we traveled northward, the herds of animals became numerous. We became expert hunters of woolly mammoths, reindeer, elk, deer, and bison. The musk oxen and woolly rhinoceroses were mean and fierce; we left them alone. We never found another truly pleasant valley. It grew colder as we traveled north. We learned to hunt and work together to survive. It became so cold that our tents no longer provided enough protection. Saber-toothed tigers, hyenas, and wolves were attacking us. We looked hard to find a good cave for protection from the weather and animals. Strong winds could not blow caves down as they did our tents. After a long time we found this beautiful valley. Now we have plenty of fresh water, enough plants for food, and many different animals to hunt. Our biggest problem is the cold weather. But we have been on many hunts, so we have furs to keep us warm. God provided well for us. I was a small boy when we arrived here, and now I am an old man."

Jabeth looked around him. Grandfather was right. Jabeth was grateful for his strong, comfortable home. He was proud of the fur clothes Mother had made for him. When it was especially cold and windy, the family spent many happy days by the fire telling stories.

29

The Great Wall of Ice

"Grandfather, when did you first see the Great Wall of Ice?" Jabeth asked.

"When we first settled in our valley, my father, older brothers, and I were stalking a herd of reindeer. On the fourth day we saw what looked like a white mountain in the distance. The herd tried to escape by running toward it, but the ice cliff blocked their escape. Because of the Ice Wall we had a successful hunt.

"The Ice Wall looked like a huge hulking white monster. Strong, cold winds blew off it into the valley. Streams of muddy water gushed out from under it. The bottom of the ice wall was imbedded with rocks.

"We decided to be brave and climb up onto the ice mountain. Long, deep cracks ran through the ice. We walked up to one and looked down. We couldn't see the bottom. The hard-packed snow created a wide ridge that went toward the North Star as far as we could see. Constant cold winds were blowing so hard that we could hardly hear each other speak. Suddenly, we heard a loud rumble. The ground lurched under us, and we were knocked off our feet. We were terrified, thinking we had awakened a huge ice monster.

"We climbed down the ice mountain as fast as we could. Every time I recall the growl of the ice mountain; I remember the fear I felt. The ice is far stronger and greater than anything I have ever seen."

Chapter 4
The Woolly Mammoth Hunt

It was late summer—always a busy time. Much had to be done to prepare for the next winter. The women and children gathered berries and roots and dried them. After hunts, they dried the meat and tanned more furs. It was time to fill their storage places. They stored food deep in their caves and in pits. The men scouted daily for herds of bison, aurochs, reindeer, and woolly mammoths. Small animals were a delicacy for summer. Larger animals were needed for food during the long winters, so tribesmen would not have to hunt in the snow, wind, and cold.

Every fall the tribe looked forward to the woolly mammoth hunt. In colder weather, the meat spoiled less quickly. In the last several years, game had become scarce. Lathan, Naboth, Soren, Gath, and the others had to travel far from their caves in search of the herds. Two years ago they had searched all the way to the Great Wall of Ice. Yesterday Gath was trapping rabbits and spotted a herd of mammoths close to home. It was not as cold as they would have liked, but the tribesmen were afraid to wait. The herd might leave the area, so the hunt had to be planned immediately.

Woolly mammoths can be gentle animals, but when wounded, they may become very dangerous. Last year, a mammoth's heavy foot had crushed a man from a neighboring tribe. To avoid any such injuries, the hunt had to be well-planned.

Jabeth overheard Zorak and Gath talking about starting the hunt the next day. They couldn't drive the animals into the usual muddy areas, called bogs, which were normally used for hunting, because they were too far away. The men were afraid that they might lose the animals before they reached there, though the bogs were normally excellent for trapping. Animals that became stuck in the mud were easy targets for spears. This time the men planned to herd the animals up a large hill, and force them to jump off a cliff. Animal jumps had been successful when hunting horses and bison. Would the jumps work for the mammoths? The men discussed using drums to frighten the hairy elephants up the hill. Zorak worried that the mammoths might stampede the wrong way and trample someone.

Jabeth had an idea. He remembered how animals feared fire. So he suggested that the men use fire to make them run in the right direction, over the cliffs. The summer had been unusually dry and warm so Gath thought the idea would be too dangerous. "What if the fire rages out of control and spreads over the grass land?" he asked. If that occurred, the animals would have a difficult time finding food and surviving the winter. Soren was worried that someone might be burned. After some discussion, Jabeth's father thought of a way to keep the fire under control. They would clear a wide strip of ground that the fire could not jump over—a firebreak. Everyone needed to work quickly to clear the strip of all grass and plants before the animals came.

The tribesmen struggled most of the day stripping away brush and weeds. They cleared a wide dirt path that the fire couldn't jump. It went from one side of the hill to the other. Then they stacked wood on the cliff side of the firebreak for the fires.

Lathan planned to light the wood piles after the mammoths crossed the break. "Can we check the progress of the herd?" Jabeth and his friends asked Lathan after most of the work was done. They found the animals a short distance from the firebreak. Twenty mammoths were contentedly grazing on the late summer grass. Jabeth ran to inform his father. Lathan called the people together and gave them final instructions.

The next morning, ten of the men left to herd the mammoths toward the cliffs. A second group was to stay near the firebreak with fire sticks and spears. Lathan assigned the third group to wait at the bottom of the cliffs. Their job was to kill the

wounded animals. The women and children stood near the third group to skin and butcher the meat quickly so it would not spoil. Jabeth's heart pounded with excitement. He hoped his plan would work and no one would get hurt.

Jabeth's group formed a half-circle around the far side of the mammoths and gently coaxed them forward. They were slowly munching their way toward the cliff. Some looked up curiously for a moment, but then moved to the next grass clump with the rest of the herd. Several hours later, the mammoths were close to the firebreak.

Suddenly, one of the animals smelled smoke from the fire sticks. His head and trunk rose to trumpet a warning. Jabeth thought quickly. He and the other boys shouted and banged their drums to frighten the animals closer to the cliffs and past the firebreak. It worked. Most of the mammoths broke out of the trap, but six of them were far enough inside for the men to start the fires. Lathan lit the first brush pile. The other men helped, and then chased the mammoths with their spears. The raging fire frightened the animals away from their escape route. They stampeded and ran toward the cliff. In the confusion, four mammoths ran off the cliff. The other two broke through the fire line and ran free with slightly scorched coats. Below the cliff, the men quickly speared the wounded animals. Jabeth's family did not want them to suffer. The women and children quickly moved in and began butchering. The plan worked better than expected. No one was hurt, and they would eat well this winter.

Cave Art and Stone Tools

The mammoth feast lasted for four days. There were games, plenty of food, and exciting stories. Even with the festivities and work, there was an underlying sadness in the air. Their Beetle-Brow friends were moving on after the celebration. Unlike Jabeth's tribe, they never settled long in one place. The Beetle-Brow people knew they had to leave before winter set in. The land could not support both tribes.

On the morning of the third feast day, Jabeth, Baylock, and his younger brother, Jubal, sat at the entrance of their cave playing a game of marbles. They were using some pretty agates and round painted rocks. They overheard their uncle, Soren, talking with Gath inside the cave. The men were planning to draw pictures of their mammoth hunt on the walls. This way, the unusually successful hunt would be remembered for as long as they lived in the cave. Some neighboring tribesmen thought the drawings had special power to give them good hunts. But Jabeth's tribe knew better. For them, the drawings were a way to remember God's blessings. The men were looking for a spot that wouldn't be ruined by the fire pit's smoke. They preferred a cave wall where the lumps matched the shapes of the animals they wanted to draw.

Jabeth looked at Baylock. They both ran to tell Soren about their special cave room. It was a chance to see it decorated. "Uncle Soren, we know the perfect place for your drawings. We have a cave house—a secret room way back in the cliff—that is just perfect. It has bumps, just right for the muscles of the animals."

Of the adults, only Lathan knew about the room. The boys took their uncle and Gath through a tunnel that led off from the main cave. After a while they entered a small chamber. It was only about fifteen paces in length and width. There, at the bottom of a far wall, the boys had sealed the small entrance with a rock. It would have been easy to walk right past without noticing it. Jubal rolled the rock aside. Gath and Soren looked at each other with surprise. They got down on their knees and crawled in.

"This room is very good for drawing animals," said Soren. "The air is dry and the drawings will not become smudged with soot from the fires. You were right, the lumps are in the right spots. Thank you for telling us about this room." The boys were proud to have their secret room decorated with such exciting art.

Gath went back into the main cave to gather and mix his paints. Red ocher was his favorite color. It was the color of blood, so it had a special meaning to the tribe. Jubal asked Gath, "Why is ocher a special color?" "Life is in the blood," Gath told him. "Because red ocher is the color of blood, it is perfect for depicting the life and death of the animals we hunt." He mixed his colors from plants and special types of soil. Next to him lay the moss, chewed twigs, and feathers that Soren would use as paint brushes. Soren's favorite was an air brush made from a hollow reed.

Soren started his work on the cave house wall. He was considered the best artist among the cave dwellers. He marked the wall with long, strong strokes and took time to decide where each line was going to be placed. Jabeth and Baylock stood in awe as a woolly mammoth began to take shape. After the animal was outlined, Soren filled in the colors. When he finished, he used the reed airbrush to sign the drawing with his hand print, using his favorite color. Jubal asked Gath if he could use any leftover paint to color his rock-marble collection. Gath was very generous, so Jubal happily set to work.

There Was Always Work to Do

The rest of the clan was busy, too. Living as hunters in a cave was work as well as fun. They needed to use all their resources wisely. Bones that were not useful for tools and art were stockpiled in a small chamber to the side of the cave. The bones would be burned during the winter when they ran out of wood. Such fires needed a lot of air to become hot enough to burn bones. These special fire pits had small air tunnels built underneath to bring in the air.

Long, curving mammoth tusks served many purposes. Zorak carved on an ivory tusk as Jabeth watched and learned. Jabeth was proud that Zorak was willing to teach him. Knives and other tools were made from tusks and bones. Zorak fashioned needles for sewing and jewelry for ceremonies. He saved the best ivory for bird sculptures. He was well-known among the neighboring tribes for his beautifully designed birds. They were in great demand for trading. Soren carefully aimed a rock to chip a piece of flint into an arrowhead. He then finished a new scraper for cleaning hides. He had become so expert that his flint edges were very sharp.

Myra helped her friend Listra sew some tanned skins into large sheets. Listra was newly married and needed many things.

Jabeth remembered Grandfather had told him that before Noah's Flood, people used melted rocks to make tools. For a while after the Flood, they continued to make melted-rock tools. But now no one remembered how. These tools lasted much longer than plain rock tools. Jabeth decided to try an experiment. He asked Grandfather about it. "I tried it when I was young and I failed. But go ahead and try," Grandfather said. So Jabeth gathered several different kinds of rocks. He knew that they had to become very hot to melt, so he used the extra-hot fire pit, the one that had air tunnels under it. He placed one rock at a time in the fire to see what would happen. Some rocks cracked, and some just turned red, but none melted. Jabeth was disappointed and so were his friends. They all had thought it was a good idea. Jabeth and the elders decided that maybe he hadn't found the right kind of rock. Had the fire been hot enough to work? Jabeth decided to keep trying. He told the elders that when he became a man, he would find rocks that melted so everyone could make strong tools.

Chapter 5
Beetle-Brow Wanderings

The next day, Jabeth noticed that Ungar, leader of the Beetle-Brow tribe, wasn't busy. He had been wondering about the places his new friends had lived in before they came to his valley. He walked over and asked him a question. Trying to use words he thought the tribesman would understand, he asked: "What is it like far away?" Ungar shook his head. Fortunately, Grandfather was nearby. Since Ungar hadn't understood Jabeth's question, Grandfather translated. Ungar took off his bear skin and sat down. He loved to tell stories to children. The other children had finished their work, and soon Ungar had a large audience, which pleased him.

As Ungar spoke, Grandfather repeated after him. "My father's father and many before him told this story to their sons. Long, long ago, we left the land of two rivers, the land that had the high tower. Our tribes traveled toward the North Star. We kept moving, never settling more than a few days in any one place. Twelve moons later, we arrived here. The weather was milder then. There was much more rain and snow. The Wall of Ice was smaller than it is now. Summers were cooler and the winters were mild. Many animals lived here. We hunted on the days when the dark ash was thinner. We ate well.

"Our tribe liked to wander. When we became too large, we divided into smaller groups. Some left here, but we stayed. Later, another clan passed back through here. They said they'd been living in the land of the setting sun. They found different animals there that were good to eat. That clan spoke of warmer winters. They also spoke of a great expanse of water with crashing waves.

"We were bored here. The new land sounded very exciting. We wanted to experience new adventures and to hunt new animals. So we journeyed toward the setting sun. A mighty lake with gigantic waves crashing onto the sand

stopped us. Although we had heard stories of this lake, it was larger than anything else we'd ever seen. The water was warm and salty. We tried to drink it, but it made us sick. Birds wheeled in the air looking for fish in the water below. It was foggy and misty much of the time. We followed the lake in the direction of the North Star, which peeked through the dark clouds once in a while. The lake seemed endless.

"We hunted a strange, furless but delicious animal that lived in rivers and small lakes. The animal had fat, short legs, a large, round body, and weighed many stones. He was easy to hunt and kept us well fed. We named him hippopotamus. There were many rivers and streams in those days. We hunted the hippopotamus, along with reindeer, the fierce woolly rhinoceros, the woolly mammoth, and a large deer with huge horns."

Ungar bent down and drew pictures of these animals in the dirt. The children were delighted.

Ungar continued his story, "While we lived along the salt lake, the air gradually became colder, but the water remained warm. At first we thought the change was temporary, so we continued hunting there. Hippopotami became fewer and fewer. Then they disappeared. The mountains and the northland became filled with snow and ice. The sky was still very dark. We left and headed in the opposite direction of the North Star, but stayed close to the mighty lake.

Musk Ox

Giant Elk

Woolly Rhinoceros

Hippopotamus

Crocodile

"After two moons, our ancestors came to a large, rock mountain along the lake. In the direction of the setting sun there was only water. In the direction of the rising sun there was only water. But to the south there was land on the other side of a salty river. They wanted to cross, but it looked very dangerous. Water was rushing through the channel between a rock mountain and the distant shore. After much thought my people decided to build strong, heavy rafts. It required a lot of work. They all made it safely to the other side. There they found a land of many rivers, fresh lakes, and much game. My ancestors often spoke of dragons in the rivers. They had large, long mouths and many sharp teeth. Their tails were strong and powerful; one swish could break a man's bones. They called the dragons crocodiles. They named the new land Saharia, and hunted there many moons.

"In time, the rain stopped and the land became dry. In the rivers and pools, the fish lay dying. Because of the stories their ancestors had told about good hunting in the direction of the North Star, they retraced their steps. Eventually, the tribe arrived back at the Great Wall of Ice."

The Ice is Melting

Jabeth and his family had enough food to share with the Beetle-Brow clan. The Beetle-Brows had helped in the hunt by working on the firebreak. Extra meat would help them on their journey.

While the women and the young girls prepared to celebrate the successful mammoth hunt, Jabeth gathered firewood with Grandfather for the cave fire. He was still glowing with excitement from the hunt and questions kept crossing his mind. Father said many herds had roamed the area when he was a boy. Ungar said game had always been plentiful. Where had the animals gone? A few weeks ago, when Lathan scouted for mammoth herds near the Ice Wall, he'd noticed a bare hill projecting from an ice flow. That hill hadn't been visible two years earlier. The ice withdrew more each year. Jabeth wanted to know why it was melting so fast. Would the ice wall still be there when he grew old? Now that he had Grandfather all to himself, Jabeth began to ask him questions.

The two sat on a large log. Bright sunlight reflected off a small stream in the sparse woods. What a pleasant day!

Grandfather thought for a minute. "Jabeth, I, too, have often wondered why the ice is melting. Weather has changed since I was a boy. Summers then were cold and wet. The days were often dim. Now we rarely see black clouds of ash. The sun warms the land more. Other wandering tribes say the summers are becoming warmer everywhere. Many days' walk away from the North Star, large lakes are drying up. My ancestors told of a large lake two moons from the Tigris-Euphrates rivers, toward the setting sun. Ungar says the last he heard, the lake had shrunk and become salty. Fish no longer live in that lake. They now call it the Dead Lake.

"Summers are warming up; winters are becoming even colder. I remember winters full of snow and rain, but they were not as cold. Now they are dry and bitter. Every year it changes more. I believe if this continues, the Great Wall of Ice may soon melt. We may not get enough snow to make up for the summer's melting. The winter storms are different, too. Their winds pick up large amounts of dust that sometimes stays in the air for days. Ungar says dust is piling up many-men-high not too far from here. He once saw a sick bison buried in a dust storm.

"The valley rivers are swollen from the melting ice. Summer floods have become enormous in the past five years. One day, I saw a herd of bison drinking along the river. Suddenly, the high river bank behind them broke off and slid down over the animals, burying them. It was awful. The other day Zorak saw a horse caught in raging flood waters. Many animals are being killed in flooding rivers; other animals are moving away. All nature is in turmoil. Maybe we will have to move again to find better hunting. I dread the thought. I am not sure my old body could take a move. Right now, it is too dangerous to go; there is too much flooding in the lowlands. We are safe here in our caves for now, and plan to remain here a while longer. We trusted God in the past, so we'll continue to believe that He'll provide us with food and show us what to do."

Grandfather and Jabeth continued talking. The sun sank behind the distant hills, and light rays fanned out through red- and orange-colored clouds.

Woolly Mammoths in Siberia

As the children took one of their last walks together they discussed how many animals would be left for them to hunt when they grew up.

"Grandfather told me yesterday," Jabeth said, "that large animals, especially mammoths, are disappearing everywhere. Earlier this summer Grandfather spoke with a tribe passing through our valley. They came from the direction of the North Star and the rising sun. Many mammoths used to roam there too. So did elk, reindeer, woolly rhinoceros, horses, deer, and bison. The wandering tribe called their land Siberia. To the north of that land is a big salty lake. They called the lake Arctica. South of Siberia, there is another salty lake called Pacifica. The tribe lived in that far-away land for many moons.

"As here, their weather was changing. Warm, gentle winds often blew from the warm Arctica and Pacifica Lakes onto the land. Siberia received only a little snow during the winter. It rained much in the summer. Mist rose from the salty lakes and formed big rain showers that watered all the land. Grass and flowers were plentiful so the animals were fat and sleek.

"Grandfather said that after many moons, it gradually grew colder. Winters became so cold that the ground stayed frozen a few feet below the surface even during the summer. Water from the melting snow couldn't soak into the soil. It pooled, forming large, muddy bogs. Grass and flowers began disappearing. In the summer, large rivers swelled with water and mud.

"Soon, animals left the area. First, the elk and deer moved out, then the bison and horses disappeared. Some of the animals went the way of the rising sun. They passed through a land called Alaska and on down into a wide, spacious land. Some people from other tribes that followed the animals returned and told about the new land.

"Woolly mammoths are stubborn. Once they like an area, they usually stay. They must think their shaggy coats can keep them warm in any weather. The woolly mammoths gradually moved closer to Lake Arctica, where winters weren't so cold. They found more food. They passed around the bogs. At the same time, the tribe braved the cold. Chasing woolly mammoths back into the bogs was easy, and meat was plentiful.

"Suddenly, late one summer, a large storm blew in, and Lake Arctica quickly froze over. Then the air became very cold. The hairy elephants panicked. Some ran away from the frozen lake. They became trapped in the bogs which now covered the land. Many of them drowned in the flooded rivers and were rapidly buried along the mud banks. Cliffs along the rivers caved over other mammoths, just like the one Grandfather saw. As it became even colder, a few of the buried animals were frozen very quickly.

"So many animals died that the people did not have enough food to live. They had to leave quickly. They headed toward the setting sun. Hunger and cold stalked them like an enemy. Some died and others barely made it out of Siberia alive. As they traveled away from the North Star, the hunting was better and the weather warmer. By the time they passed through our region they were healthy again. We shared some of our dried meat and roots with them. I wonder what it all means? The mammoths have died out in Siberia. They are dying out here. Will there be any mammoths left for us to hunt when we grow up?"

"I surely hope so," said one of the Beetle-Brow children.

The Beetle-Brows Depart

Do you know where your tribe is going now?" Jabeth asked his Beetle-Brow friend.

"We're going to go back to a land where the hunting is better and the winters aren't as cold. We're going to miss you and your clan. It has been fun playing together. I don't know when we can come back, now that there is less meat here. We will have to go somewhere else to hunt the big animals," he said sadly.

The boys headed back to camp with heavy hearts. The camp was busy with the shouts and sounds of packing. Ungar was yelling directions to the women. He waved Jabeth and his friends over to help with the packing. Excitement ran high. Beetle-Brows enjoyed the adventure of moving to a new location.

Ungar and his children put all of their belongings on sleds made of poles and skins bound together. One end dragged on the ground and the other was pulled by two people. Others carried their belongings in skin packs tied to their backs.

When the Beetle-Brows were through packing, it was time for the traditional gift exchange. Lathan gave Ungar knives, spears, and some dried cave-bear meat for a going-away present. Ungar and his clan gave gifts of flint rocks, carvings, and jewelry. The morning sun warmed the air. After many sad good-byes Jabeth and his family watched them start down the valley.

Lathan then called the clan together. It was time to finish preparing for winter. He assigned each family their winter tasks. Everyone had a job to do. Jabeth was glad he was able to help his family survive in a harsh world.

Part II — Chapter 6
Life in the Great Ice Age

Jabeth and his family lived toward the end of the Great Ice Age. The end of the Ice Age was a very anxious time because of the many changes. But mankind was adaptable. After the ice sheets disappeared, the summers and winters became warmer. The weather eventually became as it is now. The gigantic dust storms ended. Trees became abundant. Unfortunately, many of the large herds of animals disappeared. Some animals became extinct, but others survived and returned to northern and central Europe. Since the weather was warmer, Jabeth, his children, and grandchildren moved from their caves into tents. They eventually built houses, and later cities as the population increased. Farming became a way of life. They discovered the lost art of mining and making metal tools. Because life was much easier than the last few hundred years of the Ice Age, civilization took a giant leap forward.

A Different Climate

During the first half of the Ice Age, the combination of warm oceans and cold land would have caused a different climate than today. Land close to the warm ocean would have been pleasantly warm. Warm, moist air off the Atlantic Ocean would have constantly bathed countries like France, Spain, and England. This is why Ungar's tribe was able to find and hunt hippopotami, which require plenty of river water and a warm place to live. In southern England scientists were puzzled when they found hippopotamus bones mixed with bones of animals that loved the cold, such as the woolly rhinoceros, mammoth, reindeer and musk ox. The unique climate after the Flood can explain why the hippopotami lived so far north during the early Ice Age. A warm Atlantic ocean would spread warm moist air into western Europe.

Jabeth and his family lived in central Germany, just south of the Great Wall of Ice. The Neanderthal people lived in that region well before Jabeth's family. Ungar's ancestors remembered that the snow and ice on the ice sheet had been much thinner early in the Ice Age. The ice gradually built up year after year. The early winters were warmer in this region than the winters during Jabeth's time. Warm breezes blew off the Atlantic Ocean, but cooled as they continued inland to Germany. Early in the Ice Age, summers would have remained cool and dark. There was probably only a small temperature difference between summer and winter.

The Neanderthals probably found the overwhelming amounts of rain and snow depressing. It rained heavily for days on end. When it snowed, it continued as though it would never end. Since the weather was nasty and it was dark most of the time, Neanderthals stayed in their cave homes as much as possible. Because of this, they likely developed a disease called rickets. Rickets causes bones to become so soft that legs become bowed. Soft bones also break easily. The lack of sunshine, along with a poor diet, probably contributed to the beetle-brow look. Some of their unique features could also have been just a family trait like big ears, or a long nose. Because Neanderthals looked different from people today, some scientists referred to the Neanderthal people as a "missing link." All that has changed. Now scientists realize Neanderthals were as human as we are.

Because so much more rain and snow fell during the Ice Age, large lakes existed. Many of them are now dry basins, or salt lakes. The Dead Sea, which Ungar called the Dead Lake, was once much larger and filled much of the Jordan River Valley of Israel. In North America, many lakes covered the hot dry areas of Nevada, Utah, and southern California. The Great Salt Lake was about 800 feet deeper then, and 17 times bigger. There was even a lake in Death Valley, California! These basins were originally filled with water from the Genesis Flood. The wetter climate during the Ice Age would have kept them high for a long time.

Even the Sahara Desert, one of the hottest and driest places on earth, was much wetter not long ago. Ungar's ancestors told of crossing into the Sahara Desert (Saharia) from the rock of Gibraltar in southern Spain. In fact, fossilized remains of the Neanderthals were found at Gibraltar. Rock art and abundant human artifacts have also been found in North Africa. When Ungar's ancestors saw the Sahara, it was not a desert. It had rivers and streams and many plants. Crocodiles (dragons to Ungar's tribe) made the rivers dangerous. Would you believe the evidence for this much wetter climate lies below the desert sands? Special satellite radar has spotted dried-up rivers and lakes. Evolutionary scientists don't understand why large lakes and rivers once snaked through the Sahara. Fossils of crocodiles,

as well as fossils of clams, hippopotami, buffaloes, elephants, giraffes, and many other animals have been found there. These fossils prove that North Africa, at one time, was very different from the desert it is today. This much wetter climate was fairly recent. We know this because live crocodiles have been found in some of the shrunken lakes of the western Sahara. Crocodiles do not travel on hot desert sand. They are remnants of the wetter climate that existed during the Ice Age.

Painting Materials and Techniques

The illustration on page 37 shows the creation of a cave painting. Ice Age artists mixed the colors used in their paintings from natural earth pigments. Made from minerals, these colors are permanent. Ocher, a clay that contains iron minerals, was the most common material used.

Depending upon its chemical content, ocher can range in color from intense yellow and bright, blood-red to dark, deep tans and browns. Blacks were made from burned charcoal, but they were

51

not as permanent as blacks made from another mineral—manganese oxide. To make paints, these various natural materials were first crushed and ground between rocks to a fine powder. Then they were mixed with different kinds of liquids, such as plant, fruit, and vegetable juices, as well as egg white, blood, and animal fat. The artists applied these paints to the cave walls with brushes made of animal hair, chewed twigs, feathers, and moss. The most unusual tool was an "air brush" made from a length of hollow reed or a hollow bird bone. The Ice Age artist blew powdered pigment through such a tube to leave the stenciled imprint of his hand. This may have been a personal signature on a work of art, or quite possibly, meant to leave a record of his existence.

Painting by the Light of Stone Lamps

Ice Age artists working deep in caves would have created their paintings by artificial light. No doubt they used torches made of sticks and/or plant fiber. But the beautifully crafted stone lamp

illustrated here, found in Lascaux Cave, in France, shows just how advanced these artists were. Moss or locks of hair served as wicks for these cup-like lamps that were hollowed out of stone and fueled with animal fat. Several of these slow-burning lamps may have been used to light the cave. A great deal of planning had to go into everything they did. A similar lamp is pictured on page 37.

Ice Age Jewelry and Bird Carvings

As they do today, people in the Great Ice Age enjoyed wearing different kinds of jewelry. Men, women, and children wore such decorative items as necklaces, bracelets, and pendants. The jewelry illustrated in this book are all based on actual historical artifacts some of which are reproduced here.

The necklace at the top of the illustration, constructed of shells and fox teeth, was worn in Ice Age Europe. It is from the collection of the Anthropos Moravske Museum in Brno, Czechoslovakia.

The bottom necklace was found by Russian anthropologists in an Ice Age burial site at Mal'ta, near Lake Baikal in Siberia. Carved of mammoth ivory, the pendant is an example of a fairly common carved image—a migratory water

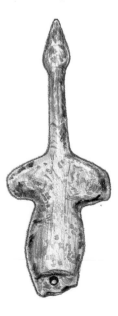

bird in flight. Some bird images were highly abstract, such as the large pendant piece pictured at the bottom of the illustration. It's the main decorative element in this beaded necklace.

Other bird images were more realistic such as the long-necked pendant piece (previous page, bottom right) representing either a goose or duck. Similar bird carvings are shown in the illustration on page 38.

Ice Age experts point out that birds were not the primary animal food source for Ice Age hunters, who relied mainly on mammals. Some experts suggest that Ice Age carvings of migratory birds were symbols of the arrival of spring and new life. Perhaps their use in personal adornment and placement with the dead at burial sites relates to mankind's belief in resurrection and an eternal life.

Cave Tent Shelters

The clammy cave dwellings of Ice Age men were often chilly and uncomfortable. For additional warmth and privacy, families lived in separate tent shelters like those shown in the illustration on page 9.

Postholes found on the floor of a cave in southern France provides evidence that these tent-like shelters were sapling tree trunks braced against a ridgepole. The top painting shows the horizontal ridge pole that was supported at each end by a vertical pole rising from a hole dug into the cave floor. Side support poles were leaned against the ridge pole and tied to it. The middle painting shows how the tent shelter's wood frame was covered with layers of animal skins that were placed like the overlapping shingles on the roofs of today's homes. The skins were lashed to the wooden poles with plant or leather strips. The bottom painting shows how piles of rocks were placed to seal off drafts and to anchor the lowest layer of animal skins to the cave floor.

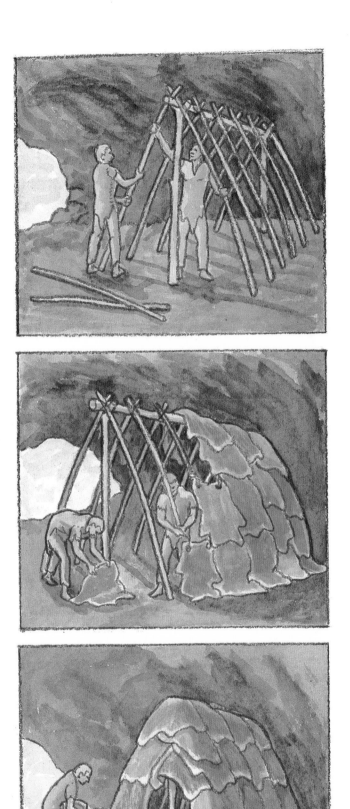

Ice Age Cave Art

The illustrations in this book show some of the animals that have been depicted in paintings, drawings, and sculpture by Ice Age artists. The illustration on page 24 and 25 shows a cave painting of a bison, representative of the great herds that roamed the grasslands of Europe during the Great Ice Age. Some of these beasts had horns up to four feet wide. Hunting these animals for their meat and hides must have been dangerous.

Another awesome creature found in Ice Age art was the 12-foot-long aurochs—or wild bull—known as the ancestor of all domestic cattle. It stood almost six feet at its shoulder. The powerful, dangerous, and swift aurochs were the original "cattle kind." From the population of seven aurochs in the Ararat region (Genesis 7:12), many different cattle breeds have developed over the centuries. The last aurochs died in 1627 in Poland. The Ice Age painting above this illustration of the aurochs is based on an original work discovered in the Lascaux Cave in France. A similar painting is shown in the illustration on page 11.

The horse was a popular subject for Ice Age artists, as well. The wild horses depicted in Ice Age art were small and stocky. They had short, stiff manes and rather shaggy hair. These horses were killed by men both for food and for use of their skins. One of the most beautiful examples of sculpture inspired by the wild horse is this three-inch-long carving of mammoth ivory from France. The horse's stiff mane and coarse, hairy coat have been carefully rendered by tiny scratches in neatly patterned rows. Similar sculptures are shown on pages 38 and 48.

The leaping horse sculpture—about a foot long—was carved from a reindeer antler discovered in Bruniquel, France. Some experts have identified it as a spear thrower. Spear throwers were used to help project a spear a greater distance with greater force. The two men on the right hand side of the cave bear hunt illustration, page 23, are using spear throwers. One of the reindeer hunters on page 31 is also holding a spear thrower. The small size and fine workmanship of this particular carving may indicate, however, that it was not actually used for hunting, but was a ceremonial object perhaps used to commemorate or celebrate a successful hunt.

Stone Age Tools

The perforator (below left) was used to punch holes in leather because the hide was too tough for needles. First, the holes were punched, then the clothing was stitched together using the bone needles threaded with sinew. The perforator was also used to drill holes in wood, bone, and antler. It was used to put the "eye" in bone needles. Myra is using a perforator on page 39.

The burin (above right) was a sharp knife-like tool made from flint. Small chips of flint were knocked off, using a hammer of bone or antler, until the edge was nearly as sharp and efficient as any steel knife today. The razor-sharp tool allowed Ice Age man to do many tasks that would have been much harder or impossible without it. It could cut any material softer than it was.

With it tools and weapons could be made from antlers, ivory, and animal bones. A burin was used to make sewing needles, harpoons, spear throwers, and jewelry. It was also used as a cutting tool for hides and meat. On page 26 a burin is used to slice cave bear meat.

Bone Needles

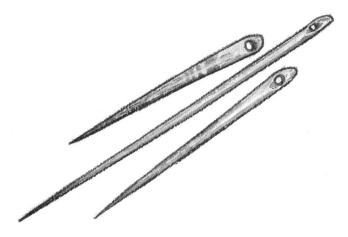

Needles were made using a burin, an antler, and a stone with a groove in it. First the antler was softened in water. Then a triangular shaped piece was removed and the shaping begun. It was rubbed against a piece of stone to thin it down and sharpen it. When it was thin enough, a hole was bored with a perforator. The longest needle (life size) is four inches long. Mother is using a bone needle on page 11.

Ice Age Musical Instrument

This bird-bone flute is pictured in the cave bear hunt celebration on page 24. The first mention of musical instruments is in Genesis 4:21. It would seem people have had an appreciation for music from the very beginning.

Stone Hearth

Archaeologists have discovered many ingenious ways Ice Age man solved the problem of living as comfortably as possible in a harsh climate. Limited resources and very short summers must have made any progress difficult. One example of this is the tent-like shelters, shown on page 9, that were constructed inside caves for warmth, safety, and privacy.

Preserving and preparing food would have been major concerns. Storage pits, close to their cave homes, were dug in dry ground and lined with rocks. To keep the food safe from prowling bears, wolves, and other animals a stone slab covered the pit. Meat and other foods were kept frozen in the pits through the long Ice Age winters. One of the delicacies kept in these pits was frozen berries.

Other common foods were nuts, fruits, bulbs, roots, and seeds. Nuts could be eaten right out of the shell or ground into a powder and mixed with other foods as Mother did on page 20.

Food preparation was another problem. One solution was discovered at Pech de l' Aze in southern France. A large flat rock hearth was found that showed signs of repeated heating. Jabeth's mother may well have used this same technique to prepare food for her family. See pages 9 and 20.

On a large hearth of flat rocks (top) Mother built a fire to heat the rocks. After the rocks were heated, she used a long paddle-like stick (middle) to push the red-hot coals off to one side. The hearth is now hot enough (bottom) for her to prepare the family's meal

Along with the stone griddle, cooking pits were also used as shown on page 27. A small hole was dug in the ground approximately one- to two-feet wide and a little over a foot deep. The pit was lined with a thick flexible hide held in place with wooden pegs.

Saber-Toothed Tiger

The authors and artists who created this book have used artistic license by including a type of large saber-toothed cat. Although remains of these large cats have not been found in Europe, they are one of the best-known Ice Age animals.

Fossils of a massive "cave lion," *Felis leo spelaea*—one third larger than any living lion—have been found in central Europe. But the saber-toothed tiger is usually the cat identified, by most people, with the Ice Age.

The scientific name of the saber-toothed tiger is *Smilodon,* which means "knife tooth." *Smilodon* was a large cat, about 10 feet long from his nose to the tip of his tail. The saber-toothed tiger is best known for its spectacular six-to-nine-inch-long, sharp fangs. Slightly flattened and curved, these fangs resemble an old-fashioned type of sword, called a saber. In order to use its long, stabbing teeth, this fierce beast could drop its lower jaw down and back far enough to touch its throat. Massive neck muscles would then have allowed *Smilodon* to drive these terrible weapons into its prey.

The most impressive remains of the saber-toothed tiger have been found in the La Brea Tar Pits in Los Angeles, California. The La Brea Tar Pits are seeps of heavy oil which have formed in deep ponds of thick, sticky black tar. Water gathered in hollows of the tar pits. Animals that came there to drink found themselves trapped in the treacherous sticky tar. The remains of many plant-eating animals have also been found. Perhaps the saber-toothed tigers were attracted by other animals' struggles and then, in turn, became trapped. Several hundred *Smilodon* skeletons have been brought out of the La Brea Tar Pits.

Most of the *Smilodon* fossil remains have been found in North America, but some have also been found as far south as Argentina.

The Neanderthals

Many people today still think of the Neanderthals as primitive—a type of "Missing link" or ape man as we mentioned on pages 50 and 51. Were they really "primitive half apes"? How do they fit into the creationist's view of the past? On page 50 we have suggested reasons for their peculiar appearance based on new research. In our story, we treat them as one of the many nomadic tribes that wandered in search of food during the Ice Age. We traced one journey that Ungar's ancestors took in the pursuit of game.

When Neanderthal Man was first found in Germany and then in other countries of Europe, scientists did not know what to make of him. Some thought he was a primitive man, one of our evolutionary ancestors. Others, such as Rudolf Virchow, a famous scientist who was an expert on diseases, believed Neanderthal Man had rickets. Many Scientists today believe the same. Rickets is caused by a lack of vitamin D, from insufficient sunshine or a poor diet. In the early part of the twentieth century, an expert on fossil man, Marcellin Boule, made the Neanderthal Man look ape-like by giving him him a stooped appearance. He made his big toe point outward and portrayed him walking with bent shoulders.

Modern experts realize that Dr. Boule made many mistakes. Neanderthal's big toe was human and not like an ape, and he did not shuffle along bent-kneed. Scientists have found over 200 individuals of Neanderthal Man all over Europe, and western Asia. Now we have a better idea what he looked like. Many evolutionary scientists have concluded that the Neanderthal Man is not a "missing link." He is a type of true man, like the Eskimos or the Norwegians. He stood about 5 feet, 7 inches tall and had a brain that, on average, was larger than people today.

Neanderthal Man did have a peculiar look about him. His forehead sloped backwards with ridges of bone above his eyes. The back of his

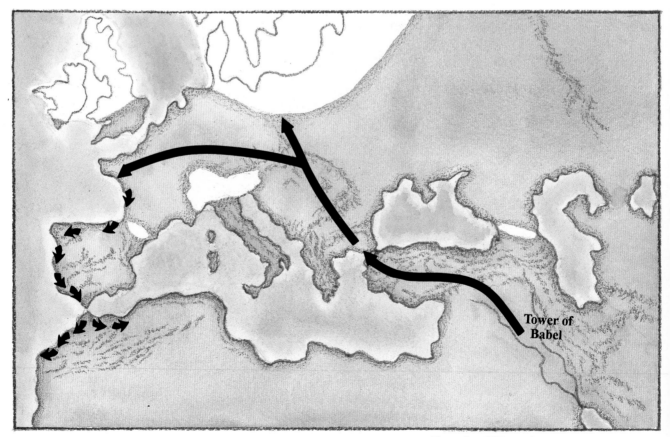

Travels of Ungar's ancestors.

head stuck out, and he had a recessed chin. This is why Jabeth's tribe called the Neanderthals, the Beetle-Brows. Neanderthal Man was powerfully built with thick bones and strong muscles. Some experts believe he was as strong as today's most avid weight lifters.

Mistaken ideas die slowly. A few evolutionists in the 1970s and 1980s still thought Neanderthal Man was primitive. They claimed he could barely talk. According to evolutionary theory, mankind had not yet evolved enough to have developed human speech. However, in 1989, researchers, in Israel, found and studied a special bone from the throat region that is related to speech. This bone was so much like the same bone in modern man that they concluded Neanderthal Man talked very well. In our story, we have Ungar telling stories to the children—just like Grandfather.

Evolutionary scientists are uncertain where Neanderthal Man originated. He and his look-alike, *Homo erectus*, appeared suddenly, just like the fossils of animals. There is no fossil evidence of any "missing-links" (transitional forms) in either the human or animal "kinds." Dogs have always been dogs; birds have always been birds; and humans have always been humans. This proves they were created and not evolved.

The sudden appearance of Neanderthal Man is a simple problem for creationists. Neanderthal Man was just one of several groups of people that spread out after the Tower of Babel. His tribe was probably more nomadic than most. Neanderthal bones are found buried in the deepest layer of cave floors. This seems to indicate that he was the first tribe to reach Europe during the worst part of the Ice Age. From western Europe, the tribe most likely crossed the Mediterranean Sea at the Rock of Gibraltar and lived in North Africa for a while. Fossils of Neanderthal Man have been found at these locations.

Evolutionists cannot agree about what happened to Neanderthal Man. They find it hard to explain his rather sudden disappearance. Some believe he was killed by the "more advanced" modern looking Cro-Magnon Man. They say Neanderthal Man was unfit to survive. But there is much evidence against this idea. Neanderthal Man was stronger and most likely as intelligent as Cro-Magnon Man. Some evolutionary scientists believe that Neanderthal Man died out before Cro-Magnons arrived on the scene. We now have a great deal of evidence that shows both groups lived in the same areas at the same time.

Many evolutionary scientists favor the theory that the Neanderthals married Cro-Magnon people and the unique Neanderthal features just phased into modern man. From the creationist point of view this is the more likely explanation. We would expect that nomadic tribes would often run into each other, especially as the population grew. Many fossils show a mix of people. There are Neanderthals that have some modern-like features, and fossils of modern people with some Neanderthal-like features. Some people living today bear a resemblance to Neanderthals. There was also a great amount of variation among the Neanderthal and Cro-Magnon tribes.

It is possible that the unique Neanderthal features were caused by the Ice Age. This was suggested on page 19 in our story. Some evolutionists agree with this idea. Fossil evidence strongly suggests the Ice Age was mostly responsible. The fossils found in western Europe are generally more Neanderthal-like than those found in southern Europe or those found farther south. This rule has exceptions which could be due to their extensive wanderings. Furthermore, many fossils of Neanderthal children do not show the Neanderthal-look as strongly. If this were true, we would expect the Neanderthals to become more modern looking after the harsh living conditions of the Ice Age were over.

The Land Bridge

After the Flood, the animals released from the Ark rapidly multiplied and migrated across the uninhabited world. To populate the entire world they had to cross from one continent to another. We know that many animals migrated all the way to the tip of South America. Since large animals cannot swim hundreds of miles at one time, there had to have been land bridges. A land bridge connected England to mainland Europe. We know this because many Ice Age mammals populated southern England. In addition, fossils have been found at the bottom of the English Channel and the North Sea. In just ten years 2,000 molar teeth of mammoths were dredged up from one spot in the North Sea.

In the far north there lies a shallow area of water in the northeastern Bering Sea, and the Chukchi Sea located in the southern Arctic Ocean northwest of Alaska. During the Ice Age, the shallow area formed a land bridge that connected the continents of Asia and North America. Enormous amounts of sea water were locked up in the great ice sheets which lowered the sea level. This area was likely uplifted at the same time.

Scientists have found the remains of woolly mammoths on several islands in the Bering and Chukchi Seas. Mammoth teeth have been dredged up in the shallow water around Alaska. This is good evidence to prove that a land bridge once connected the continents.

Siberia and northern Alaska were much warmer during the Ice Age than they are today. The animals would have been fairly comfortable as long as they didn't try to cross the glaciers. There were ice sheets covering the mountains of Alaska. Besides being cold and windy, the ice sheets provided little food. If they hadn't found a route around the ice, they would have been trapped in Alaska until the ice melted.

Glacial geologists discovered a corridor that received very little snow, east of the Rocky Mountains from northwest Canada to Montana. This area was glaciated during only part of the Ice Age. Two weather conditions caused this to happen. First, the Rocky Mountains are far from the oceans, so they received light snowfall. Second, the chinook winds off the Rocky Mountains would dry and warm the air. "Chinook" is a Native American term meaning "snow eater." These winds would keep the corridor free of ice for quite awhile. As a result, there was a pathway for the animals between the Rocky Mountain ice sheet and the ice sheet well east of the mountains. The large, fast animals probably found the ice-free corridor early in the Ice Age. These included the woolly mammoth, horse, bison, antelope, and even a type of camel. The slower animals, like the ground sloth and meadow mouse, would have trailed behind.

Ice Age man probably used the land bridge, as well. In northeast Siberia and north and central Alaska, several types of spears and arrow points have been found. Mankind did not colonize the earth until after the Tower of Babel. This was at least 100 years after the Flood. By the time they reached Alaska, the ice-free corridor may have been closed. If not, the temperatures were probably too cold to travel south or east. Since Siberia and northern Alaska were warmer at that time, the tribes could easily have survived in Alaska for a long time. The hunting would have been excellent.

The fact that lowland Alaska was never glaciated perplexes glacial geologists who believe in evolution. But it would be predicted in an Ice Age caused by the Genesis Flood. Warm water in the sea surrounding Alaska kept the glaciers in the mountains.

With time, the ice sheets started to melt and the corridor opened up again. So, wandering tribes—the ancestors of the Native

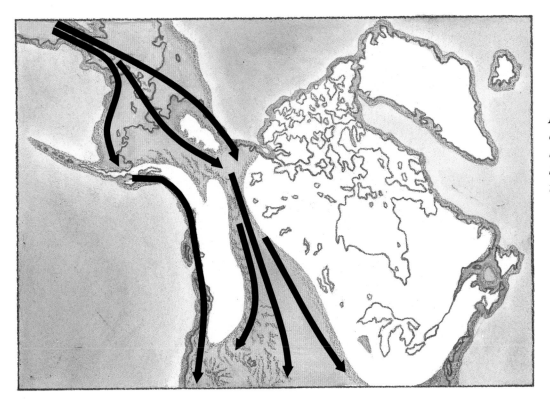

Migration routes over the land bridge between Siberia and Alaska into North America.

Americans—moved on to populate the rest of the continent. Some of the tribes enjoyed Alaska so much, they decided to stay there. They became the Eskimo and Aleut people who now inhabit Alaska, northern Canada, and parts of Greenland.

Besides using the corridor east of the Rocky Mountains, Ice Age man could have traveled down the coast of Alaska and British Columbia and continued south, into the state of Washington. The ice sheet that covered British Columbia and northern Washington state wouldn't have reached the shore until late in the Ice Age. These coastal migrants could have traveled down the Pacific shoreline either in the middle of the Ice Age or after the ice sheets retreated.

Scientists have had difficulty finding the campsites where these people may have stayed. They thought perhaps the tribes had migrated along the coast in boats. Since these islands were very close to the Pacific coastline, they would have been a natural stopping place for the tribes on their way south. Recently, a few campsites have been found on several of these islands.

In 1985, on an island just off the southeast Alaskan city of Ketchikan, archaeologists found one of these ancient camps. A prehistoric garbage dump was found filled with piles of shells and fish bones. Some of the bones were from fish that lived in water deeper than 60 feet. This evidence proves not only that early man used the Pacific route, but they also had boats and were capable of offshore fishing. Among the garbage they also found the remains of seals. This suggests these ancient people had some way to harpoon with a rope. It is impressive evidence that they were a resourceful and intelligent people. Isn't it fascinating what we can learn from garbage dumps?

While Ice Age man was trapped in Alaska or fishing down the coastline, the animals had a few hundred years' head start on repopulating the new world. So, when the corridor east of the Rocky Mountains opened up again at the end of the Ice Age, inland migrations could continue. Again, the hunting would have been excellent.

Chapter 7

The Great Ice Age

Grandfather was a good observer of nature. However, he only partially understood why the climate was changing and why the Great Wall of Ice was melting.

The Ice Age affected all the world, especially the middle and high latitudes. In Europe, glaciers developed on the mountains of Norway and Sweden. Because the nearby ocean water was warm, it took many years before these mountain glaciers spread downward into the lowlands of those countries. Eventually, as the oceans gradually cooled, the snow and ice covered all of what is now northern and central England, Denmark, northern Germany, northern Poland, and northwest Russia.

Ice covered nearly all of Canada and much of the northern United States, as well. The snow and ice extended all the way into northern Missouri.

A gigantic ice sheet eventually covered Greenland and the continent of Antarctica. Smaller ice caps covered the Swiss Alps and other mid- and high-latitude mountain ranges of the world. Volcanic dust in the stratosphere also cooled the tropics. Thus, many tropical mountains had ice caps at their summits.

Cause of the Ice Age

Over the years there have been many ideas and theories on the cause and number of ice ages. A good theory is one that best fits the physical evidence. Noah's Flood and the changes in the climate due to volcanic ash and warmer oceans best explain the cause and development of the Ice Age.

Some may think that an ice age needs colder winters. However, winters now are cold enough.

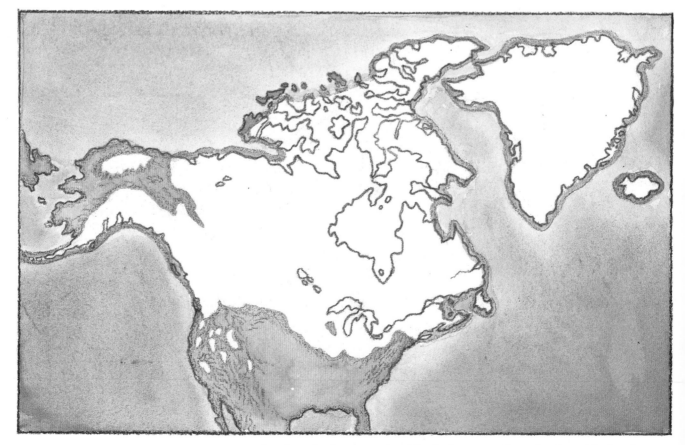

Ice Age glaciers covering North America, Greenland, and Iceland.

In present-day Siberia, winters are bitter cold, but there is no ice sheet there. What is really required is much cooler summers so the snow would not melt. Also, winters would need to be much wetter—so wet that the snow would pile high. Because of much cooler summers and more snow, the winter snow would grow deeper each year. After several years, the weight of the snow would cause it to compress and turn into ice.

You may wonder how cold such a summer would need to be. Scientists did a computer study to answer this very question. They found that ice age summers would need to be at least 20 degrees Fahrenheit colder than they are now in northeastern Canada. Farther south, in the northern United States and the lowlands of Europe where the summers are warmer, the summer temperature would have to drop even more. A summer temperature drop of at least 40 degrees Fahrenheit would probably be necessary!

Evolutionary scientists have a very hard time explaining what may have caused this drastic change. They have limited themselves to explaining the Ice Age using only present processes. What present processes could cool North American summers 20 to 40 degrees and maintain those temperatures year after year? It is understandable why over 60 theories have been invented, all with serious difficulties. A few scientists think an ice age could occur if our solar system moved through a dust cloud in the Milky Way Galaxy. Others believe that if the sun gave off less light, an ice age would occur. Of course, there is no proof for these ideas, and no way to scientifically test them.

People are worried today about a greenhouse warming due to increased carbon dioxide in the atmosphere. So, many scientists think that if the amount of carbon dioxide in the atmosphere could in some way be decreased, an ice age may develop. This method may cause cooler

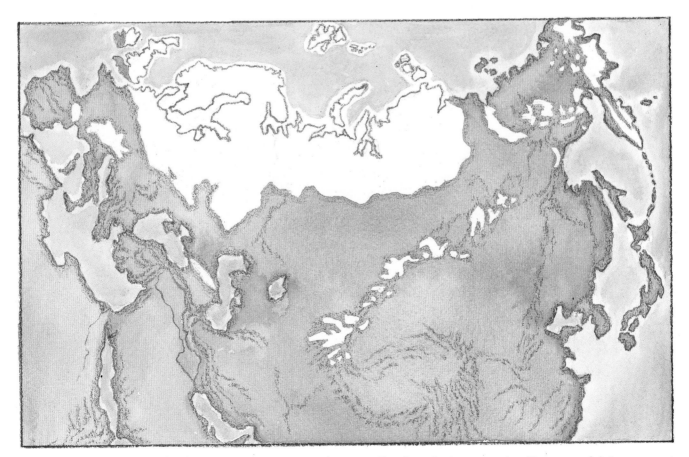

Ice Age glaciers covering Europe and Asia.

temperatures, but would not be enough for an ice age. Another idea proposed by evolutionary scientists was that raising of the mountains over millions of years caused the cooler temperatures needed for the Ice Age. The trouble with applying that theory today is that we would need summers 20 to 40 degrees cooler. Even the high mountains of today are not enough to cause an ice age.

An imaginative idea is that part of the Antarctica ice sheet spilled into the ocean. This would have spread ice and snow over a greater area of the world. More sunlight would have been reflected back into space and caused cooler temperatures. The problem with this idea is: How could more ice in the Southern Hemisphere cause an ice age in the Northern Hemisphere?

One popular theory today is called the astronomical theory. As the earth goes around the sun, the shape of the orbit changes very slightly each year. The earth's orbit around the sun is an ellipse, which is a slightly flattened circle. This shape varies with time from the slightly flattened circle to an almost perfect circle. As it does this, the amount of sunlight falling on the earth varies a little. There are two

Mount Saint Helens' eruption, May 18, 1980

other slight changes in the earth's orbit that affect sunlight; however, scientists think the change in the earth's ellipse is the most important. The change from a slightly flattened circle to a circle and back to a slightly flattened circle is calculated to take 100,000 years. The astronomical theory is really an old theory and scientists thought they had it proved once, only to find out they made a mistake. Since the mid-1970s, scientists think they have proved it again. Their "proof" is based on many evolutionary assumptions, and the scientists have neglected a lot of data. The largest problem with the theory is that changes in the earth's elliptical orbit changes the amount of sunlight by, at most, 0.17%! This is much too small for an ice age.

One evolutionary scientist said years ago that there are a lot of crazy ideas on how the ice age developed, ranging " . . . from the remotely possible to the mutually contradictory . . . "

Jabeth's grandfather was correct in believing the volcanic dust that darkened the sky was responsible for the cold. He saw that when days were dark, it was colder than when they were bright. Grandfather's ancestors said that during the Genesis Flood, many volcanoes erupted. After the Flood, the earth was unstable, and the volcanoes kept erupting. Ash and gasses from the volcanoes blasted high into the stratosphere. The ash and gasses were trapped there for a long time. Volcanic dust would have caused the colder summers by reflecting most of the sunlight back into space. One of the proofs of this volcanic activity is that, all over the earth, geologists find layers of ash. These ash beds are much thicker than the ash from the eruptions of the past 200 years.

Remember we said that an ice age also needs lots of snow? You may have wondered where all of the moisture for the snow came from. Evolutionists don't know, but creationists believe that it was a result of Noah's Flood. The surface, as well as the deep ocean, was warm for hundreds of years after the Flood. For a while, you could even swim comfortably in the Arctic Ocean! Today, the deep ocean is about 39 degrees Fahrenheit all over the world, even in the tropics. The amount of water evaporated from the warm ocean would depend on the water's temperature,

Water evaporating from the ocean

the warmer the water, the greater the evaporation rate. Immediately after the Flood, about three times more water vapor would have evaporated from the oceans than is evaporating now. Ungar's people probably noticed the mist that often rose from the ocean. Cold air from the land blew over the warm ocean water and caused rapid evaporation. You could see the mist rising. Sometimes in the fall you can see this phenomenon happening now, when a lake is still warm from the summer, and the fall air is nippy. Steam rises from the water, creating a beautiful mist. From all this water vapor, heavy snow formed and fell on the ice sheets.

You may wonder why the ocean was so warm after the Flood. The Bible says in Genesis 7:11 that in one day all the fountains of the great deep burst forth and the floodgates of the heavens opened. The "fountains of the great deep" refers

to the water that was stored beneath the earth's surface. This water is usually very hot. Today we have examples of fountains of hot water in Yellowstone National Park. Enough hot water came out of the deep to cover the mountains everywhere on earth. (The mountains before the Flood were lower than they are today. Giant earthquakes at the end of the Flood caused them to rise.) Earthquakes, storms, tidal waves, and gigantic earth movements mixed the hot water with the existing ocean water. As you can imagine, after all of this, the ocean was comfortably warm. Cold, continental air from the land combined with the warm ocean water to create a unique climate. It provided all the moisture needed for the Great Ice Age.

Old Faithful, Yellowstone National Park.

After the Ice Age began, the land temperatures cooled even more. This happened because the heavy low clouds and white snow, as well as the volcanic dust, reflected the warm sunshine back into space. Very little warm sunshine reached the ground in the area of the great ice sheets.

The Ice Melts

Grandfather and Ungar were sharp observers of nature. They were "cave men" scientists. They noticed that the climate had slowly changed during their lifetimes. Ungar remembered that the Atlantic Ocean was warmer when he was young. At the same time, he noticed it didn't rain and snow as much as it had when he was a child. They probably spent many hours by the campfire discussing this strange change in the weather. Grandfather guessed that water evaporation was cooling the ocean. Evaporation is the main cause of ocean cooling, even today. The same type of cooling occurs when you step out of a swimming pool. Even on a warm day, you can get goose bumps from evaporation.

As the oceans cooled during the Ice Age, less evaporation took place, so there was less moisture available for snow and rain. An example of how this works is that water in a tea kettle steams when it is hot. A cold tea kettle does not steam. When the water goes into the air from the ocean, it is released as snow or rain. Less water vapor in the air will cause less snow and rain to fall. If Grandfather observed less snow and rain, the ocean must have cooled a bit. The forces of nature that caused the Ice Age were winding down.

Jabeth's grandfather also observed that the sun was shining more than it did when he was a child. The earth was gradually settling down. Fewer volcanoes were erupting around the world; less volcanic ash obscured the sky. Fewer earthquakes occurred. Although their summers were warming up, summers still felt cool because cold winds blew off the ice sheet. The tribes noticed that by late summer, it was so dry they could use fire for the first time in their hunts. Now that the sun was shining more, the summers were warmer, the winters were drier, and the ice sheets began to melt rapidly. Snow and ice melt mostly by absorbing the sun's rays. The rivers that drained the ice fields filled and overflowed their banks. This caused raging floods.

Although the ice sheet was melting, Jabeth and his family had a hard life. Not only did they have to deal with the summer flooding, their winters were getting colder and colder. Although there was less snow, terrible dust storms raged. As a result, layers of dust covered the southern part of the ice sheets, causing them to melt faster. Thick layers of wind-blown dust accumulated in central North America, eastern Europe, the Ukraine, and northern China. (This rich dust is one of the reasons why crops grow so well in the American Midwest and the Ukraine.) Since the winters were so cold and miserable, the tribes had to hunt and store large amounts of food in the fall. They had to make plenty of blankets and warm clothes; but every year there were fewer and fewer large animals to hunt.

When the ice sheets were growing, there were immense herds of large animals. Plenty of grass and food grew because the rain and snow watered the land so well. Their winters were not that cold. Large animals like cool summers. However, all that changed when the ice sheets started melting. As the weather became drier, there was less food for the animals to eat. The large animals suffered the most because they needed much more food than small animals. The miserable cold caused many to migrate south, or die. In their constant search for food, some animals were swept away by raging flood waters from the melting ice, like the bison herd that Jabeth's family saw. We find many fossils in these flood sediments.

Jabeth's family was lucky to spot a herd of woolly mammoths so close. Man, the hunter, also contributed to the extinction of many large animals. (Extinct means that they disappeared everywhere on the earth.) Woolly mammoths, woolly rhinoceroses, cave bears, saber-toothed tigers, and giant elk (Irish elk) suddenly became extinct after the end of the Ice Age. Evolutionary scientists cannot explain why so many animals died. This is because they have *very different ideas* on what the Ice Age was like. The animal fossil record supports the creation point of view.

Woolly Mammoths in Siberia

Frozen woolly mammoths and millions of mammoth bones are found along the Arctic coast of Siberia and on the islands off the coast. Local villagers and ivory hunters have dug up thousands of mammoth tusks over many years. Even today they carve and sell the items they make from tusks. Some of the animals they found are so well-preserved, scientists could study what they ate before they died. Bits of buttercups, wild flowers, and grasses were stuck in their teeth and found half-digested in their stomachs.

This is all very baffling to evolutionary scientists. They believe an ice age would have been even colder than today. Siberia's winters are too cold and dry to provide food for the voracious appetite of an elephant. The summers are no better. Today, the summers in Siberia cause a vast series of muddy bogs. The bogs are a layer of gummy mud about two-feet deep with frozen ground underneath. The permanently frozen ground is called permafrost. Bogs stay wet all summer because the water from melted snow and the thawed ground cannot seep down into the permafrost. Any big-footed elephant that ventured into it would have become hopelessly stuck and died.

This mystery can be explained by the post-Flood Ice Age—an ice age that was much different from what evolutionary scientists believe happened. Instead of Siberia being colder than it is today, during the Ice Age it was actually milder and much wetter. This, as we said earlier, was because of the warm Arctic (Arctica) and Pacific (Pacifica) oceans. Warm, moist air would bathe wintertime Siberia in much warmer air than today, along with plenty

of rain. Flowers, like buttercups and grass, grew abundantly, and the animals were plentiful and well-fed.

Computer experiments have been done to discover how much warmer Siberia would become if the Arctic Ocean sea ice suddenly disappeared. Keeping the Arctic Ocean at the freezing point of sea water, the winter temperature warmed about 30 degrees Fahrenheit. The reason for this is that with no sea ice, heat and moisture from the ocean can warm the air. As we know, ocean temperatures would have been even warmer after the Flood. Consequently, Siberia would have been an ideal place for large herds of animals. Winters would be more like those on the Great Plains of North America where millions of buffalo used to roam. Summers would be warm enough so there would be no permafrost and no dangerous bogs.

Then, at the end of the Ice Age, the weather began to change everywhere. The winters became colder, summers warmer, and the air drier. Permafrost began to develop in southern Siberia. Animals and wandering tribes found it harder and harder to survive. Many of them migrated south or into North America as the climate cooled. However, the poor woolly mammoths, rather than brave the bogs of summer or migrate during the winter, moved to the warmer coast of the Arctic Ocean. For a while it was safe, since the ocean had no sea ice yet.

Ice caps had developed in the mountain ranges of Siberia. At the end of the Ice Age, these ice caps melted and the long rivers of Siberia overflowed their banks. Fresh water from the flooding rivers spread out over the Arctic Ocean. Fresh water is lighter than salt water, so it floated on top of the salt water. This was a very important event, because fresh water freezes much easier than salt water. Then, late one summer while the woolly mammoths were peacefully grazing on grass and wild flowers, an icy wind blew over the Arctic Ocean. The water near the shoreline froze first. Sunlight, instead of warming the water, reflected off the sea ice and back into space. Then the temperature fell more and the sea ice spread further out into the ocean. The air became drier.

The woolly mammoth sensed the changes. There were no more warm ocean breezes and the sea ice was increasing. They probably panicked. Many tried to flee, but were swept away by the raging dirty flood waters and quickly buried in the river bank. Others became trapped in the sticky bogs. A few were quickly buried by mud slides. By winter it had become bitterly cold and the plant food had shriveled. Drinking water became scarce. The woolly

mammoths died by the hundreds of thousands. The permafrost spread northward to the Arctic coast. Siberia has not warmed up since that time. Bones, tusks, and a few carcasses of woolly mammoths are preserved to this day.

How Long Was the Ice Age?

The length of the Ice Age can be determined by measuring how long it takes for ice sheets to grow and how long it takes for them to melt. As you recall, moisture from the warm oceans caused

Many geologists believe U-shaped valleys are usually a sign of past glacier action.

them to grow. As this moisture evaporates, it also cools the ocean. Eventually, the ocean became cool enough, and the weather dry enough, that the glaciers stopped growing. It was at that time the ice sheets started melting. If the temperature of the whole ocean right after the Flood was about 85 degrees Fahrenheit, it would take about 500 years for it to cool enough for the ice sheets to reach maximum size.

How fast the ice disappeared from the land would depend on how deep the ice was at its maximum. It is possible to estimate the depth of the ice sheet. This can be done by calculating how much water evaporated from the ocean while it was warm. Five hundred years of evaporation from a warm ocean would result in ice sheets over North America and Europe about 2,000 feet deep. Glacial geologists who accept evolution believe these ice sheets were twice this deep. The ice sheets were not uniform in thickness; some areas were much thicker than others.

Is there any evidence that the ice sheet over North America was thinner than glacier geologists believe? They have based their ideas primarily on the current size of the Antarctic ice sheet. There is no valid reason why the North American ice sheet would need to be as thick as today's Antarctic ice sheet. Scientists know that some mountains poked out of the ice. They can climb up the mountain and find how far up the mountain the ice was by the glacial debris (jumble of rocks, clay, silt, and sand) left on the slopes. They have discovered that in places along the edge, the ice was very thin. Terminal moraines—which are jumbled masses of rocks, sand, and clay—are found at the edge of the North American ice sheet. Some of these moraines are curved. By their shape and elevation above sea level, scientists confirmed that the ice was much thinner at the edge than they had previously thought.

Even if the ice was thin at the edge, the ice sheet could have been very thick farther north into Canada. Lately, scientists have discovered that the ice sheet had *several* peaks, not just one large peak over Hudson Bay. This information is based especially on the movement of rocks and finer debris that was carried by the ice sheet. An ice sheet with several peaks is thinner than one with just one peak. All this evidence supports a much thinner North American ice sheet than they

previously thought. A thin ice sheet fits better with an Ice Age after the Genesis Flood.

Grandfather was correct that Jabeth would see the Great Wall of Ice melt completely. Summer sunshine in a dry climate would cause about 30 feet of melting a year. The ice sheet in northern Germany would be thinner at the edge. If the glacier was a little less than 2,000 feet deep in northern Germany, the ice would melt in about 50 years.

In the northern countries of Sweden, Norway, and Finland, the ice would melt slower, since those countries have cooler summers than the rest of Europe. It still would melt in less than 200 years. The same principles apply to the North America ice sheet.

From these calculations, creationists conclude that the Ice Age probably lasted about 700 years all together. It took 500 years to build it, and at the most 200 years to melt it. That is a much shorter Ice Age than evolutionists believe.

Not all of the glaciers and ice sheets melted during the Ice Age. Greenland and Antarctica are too cold to melt much of anything. The Antarctica ice sheet grew to an average of 3500 feet thick during the Ice Age. This is two-thirds of the present thickness of the Antarctic ice sheet, which now is up to 10,000 feet thick. The remaining one-third of its thickness accumulated after the Ice Age. These ice sheets are a reminder of the Great Ice Age, as the rainbow is a reminder of Noah's Flood.

One Ice Age Not Long Ago

You may have been taught there were four ice ages. Scientists believed this for over 60 years. They believed evidence from many areas of the world "proved" four ice ages. Since the mid-1970s, this idea has been considered wrong. Glacial scientists now believe in at least 15, and possibly as many as 30 ice ages in a row. The ice melted completely between each ice age, they say, and the ice ages repeated regularly each 100,000 years. Where do evolutionary scientists come up with this many ice ages?

Many evolutionary scientists base their belief in multiple ice ages on the astronomical theory. We discussed this idea earlier in this chapter. They think that since the earth is old, the earth's orbital ellipse has changed regularly for millions of years. This is the reason they believe ice ages

Glacial boulder left by a retreating ice sheet.

repeated every 100,000 years. They have turned to the ocean sediments for their evidence of these many ice ages. With long tubes, they have collected sediments from the ocean bottom. Scientists base their belief in many ice ages on small changes in a few properties of this ocean sediment. These scientists make many assumptions in using ocean bottom sediments to prove the astronomical theory. One of these assumptions concerns how fast the sediment collected on the ocean bottom. To determine this, they use dating methods which are based on even

more assumptions. See how one idea, based an assumption, leads to another?

There is little evidence of many ice ages on land. Practically all of the Ice Age debris is from only one ice age. The edge of a glacier moves forward and melts back over the years. We would expect the same thing to have happened during the Ice Age. So glacial debris would sometimes be mixed with clay and dust along the edge of the ice sheet. Scientists think this mixture is evidence for more than one ice age. However, this is what we also expect with one ice sheet. Many other pieces of evidence can be gathered to show there was only one Ice Age.

Remember we said summers need to cool 20 to 40 degrees Fahrenheit to cause an ice age? It is easier to understand this much cooling with the unique climatic conditions that followed the Flood. But how could these same conditions occur 15 times in a row? In the map of North America, you may have noticed a spot of land near the Great Lakes. This area in southern Wisconsin was never glaciated. It seems much easier to explain this unglaciated area using one ice age, than many. Surely, if 15 or more ice ages occurred, one of them would have glaciated southern Wisconsin.

Woolly mammoths do not exist today. They are extinct. Do you know that at the end of the Ice Age, many large animals became extinct? This was mostly due to the climate change. If there were many ice ages in a row, you would expect large animal extinctions after each one. Scientists realize this did not happen. The evidence is consistent with only one ice age.

The Ice Age ended not too long ago. This is based on the appearance of the glacial debris. Most of the debris looks very fresh, as if it were deposited a short time ago. Streamlined grooves in the glacial debris can still be seen from the air. Around Hudson Bay, polished rocks from the ice still glisten in the sun when wet after a rain. This shows the ice disappeared a short time ago, and not about 10,000 to 15,000 years ago as evolutionists believe.

Will There Be Another Ice Age?

Many evolutionary scientists believe there will be another ice age. They believe we have had many ice ages in the past, so there will be more in the future. In fact, some believe the next ice age is due soon! In the Museum of Natural History in Washington, D.C., there is an exhibit on the Ice Age. It says half the people of the world live where former ice sheets existed. The exhibit suggests that the next ice age is not far away. A video even says: "Initiation of glacial conditions may be triggered by surprisingly rapid climate changes." Will half the world soon be swallowed up by the next ice age?

Why do you think evolutionary scientists believe another ice age is coming? Many do not believe the Bible, and they try to guess about the future. They base their ideas on what they think has happened in the past, and what is happening in the present. Signs of the recent Ice Age litter the surface of the earth at middle and high latitudes. Because of this, they believe we will have another ice age.

The Bible says the Flood in Noah's day was a one-time event. It was the Flood that disrupted the climate so much that it provided the conditions for the Ice Age. God gave us the rainbow as a promise that He will never again send a worldwide flood. Therefore, there can never be another ice age.

Dedication

We dedicate this book to our four children: David, Tara, Amy, and Nathan.

Acknowledgment

This book was a joint effort. We are very appreciative of the work done by many individuals, who dedicated themselves to see this book become a reality. We thank Earl and Bonnie Snellenberger, who not only painted the illustrations, but also went the extra mile by spending many hours researching the culture of Ice Age man. Gloria Clanin deserves special thanks for the many hours she spent designing, researching, and editing this book. We would like to thank Dr. Larry Vardiman and Marvin Lubenow for reviewing earlier drafts. Finally, we extend our appreciation to Mary Brite and Barbara Morrison for proofreading the manuscript.

Recommended Creation Science Reading

High School to Adult:

Baker, Sylvia, *Bone of Contention, (Sunnybank, Queensland, Australia: Creation Science Foundation Ltd, 1990), 35 pp.*

Gish, Duane T., *Amazing Story of Creation*, (El Cajon, California: Institute for Creation Research, 1990), 112 pp.

Gish, Duane T., *Evolution: Challange of the Fossil Record*, (El Cajon, California: Master Books, 1985), 277 pp.

Ham, Ken, *Answers Book*, (El Cajon, California: Master Books, 1991), 207 pp.

Ham, Ken, *The Lie: Evolution*, (El Cajon, California: Master Books, 1991), 168 pp.

Lubenow, Marvin L., *Bones of Contention*, (Grand Rapids, Michigan: Baker Book House, 1992), 295 pp.

Morris, Henry M., *Beginning of the World*, (El Cajon, California: Master Books, 1991), 184 pp.

Oard, Michael J., *An Ice Age Caused by the Genesis Flood*, (El Cajon, California: Institute for Creation Research, 1990), 243 pp.

Sutherland, Luther D., *Darwin's Enigma*, (El Cajon, California: Master Books, 1988), 180 pp.

Whitcomb, John C., and Morris, Henry M., *The Genesis Flood*, (Phillipsburg, New Jersey: Presbyterian and Reformed Publishing Co., 1961), 518 pp.

Children:

Fox, Norman, *Fossils: Hard Facts from the Earth*, (El Cajon, California: Institute for Creation Research, 1981), 31 pp.

Gish, Duane T., *Dinosaurs By Design*, (El Cajon, California: Master Books, 1992), 88 pp.

Ham, Ken and Mally, *D is for Dinosaur*, (El Cajon, California: Master Books, 1991), 123 pp.

Morris, John D., *Noah's Ark and the Lost World*, (El Cajon, California: Master Books, 1988), 45 pp.

Morris, John D., and Ham, Ken, *What Really Happened to the Dinosaurs?*, (El Cajon California: Master Books, 1990), 32 pp.

Parker, Gary, *Life Before Birth*, (El Cajon, California: Master Books, 1992), 85 pp.

If you would like a free *Creation Resource Catalog,* listing titles of other creation science books and videos, call or write: Master Books, P.O. Box 26060, Colorado Springs, CO 80936, 1-800-999-3777.